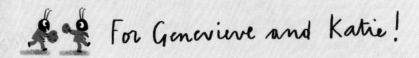 For Genevieve and Katie!

First U.S. edition 2019

Library of Congress Catalog Card Number pending
ISBN 978-1-5362-0570-1

18 19 20 21 22 23 TWP 10 9 8 7 6 5 4 3 2 1

Printed in Johor Bahru, Malaysia

This book was typeset in Providence Sans.
The illustrations were done in mixed media.

TEMPLAR BOOKS
an imprint of
Candlewick Press
99 Dover Street
Somerville, Massachusetts 02144

www.candlewick.com

templar books
an imprint of Candlewick Press

Raj
and the
BEST DAY EVER!

Sebastien Braun

Today is going to be the
BEST DAY EVER!
Dad and I are going on an adventure.

We have lots of ideas, so we make a list:

1. Borrow a book from the library
2. Go to the farm and see the tractor
3. Watch the boats go up the river
4. Look at pictures in the gallery
5. Go to the café
6. Come home on the big bus

"This is a long list," says Dad.
I say that it's the **perfect** length.

Dad and I pack our adventure bag.
"Can you think of anything else we need, Raj?" asks Dad.

I tell him that adventurers need
superhero capes,
and I put mine on.

"There's SO much
to see today!"
says Dad.

library

When we get to the library we go straight in.
I'm going to choose my **favorite** book.

OPEN
ALL THE
TIME

Dad tries to guess which one it is.
"Is it a book about a **superhero** by any chance?" he asks.

How does he **always** know?

At the library you need a special card to borrow a book,
so Dad opens his bag.

First he rummages inside. Then he tips everything onto the floor. Then he says . . .

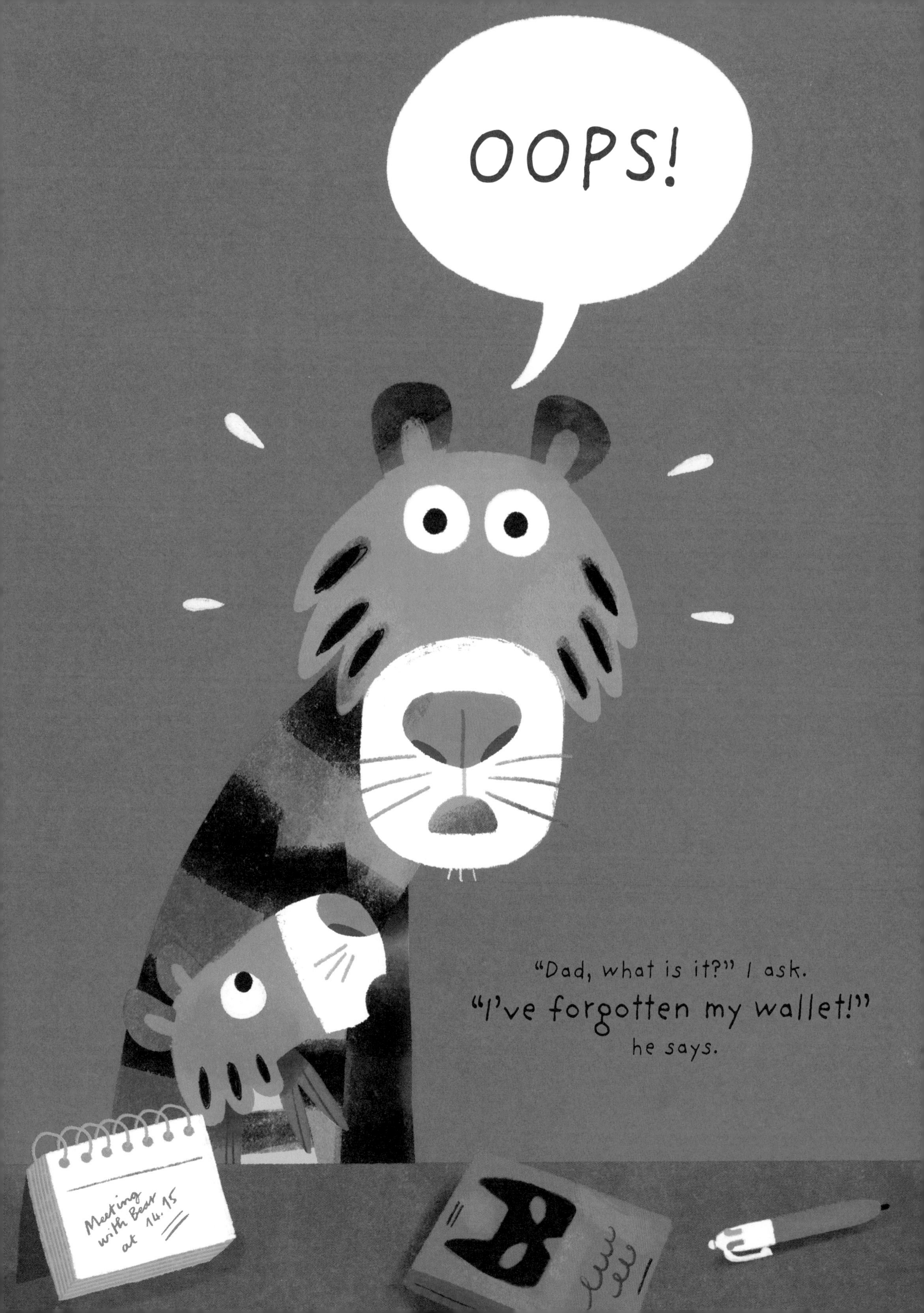

"Dad, what is it?" I ask.

"I've forgotten my wallet!"

he says.

LIBRARY

Outside it has started
to rain.
I feel rainy inside, too.
"No wallet means we
can't do all the things on
our list," says Dad.

"This is going to be the
WORST DAY EVER,"
I say back.

There is so much rain we have to run for shelter.

But then I see something that gives me an idea . . .

And I show Dad how we can drive a
shiny red tractor,
just like the one at the farm.

We have **so** much **fun** we almost don't notice
that it's stopped raining.

Next we go to the park.
Dad says he has an idea.

PARK

"Raj," he says, "can you find a leaf, a stick, and a piece of bark?"

Then Dad shows me how to turn them into a boat . . .

and we launch it!

I chase it down the stream
until it sails away.

"What should we do now?" I ask.

Dad takes out the list.
"We were going to look at pictures in the gallery."

Now I have an idea . . .

When I say I'm hungry,
Dad says, "We can't go to the café,
but we can make a picnic
right here."

So we do.

While we are eating . . .

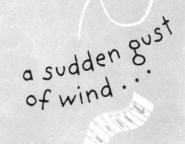

a sudden gust of wind . . .

blows the list away!

The list is stuck
in a tall tree.
"If we don't have
the list, we won't
know what to do!"
I say.

If I could fly like a
superhero,
I could get it down.

Luckily Dad is **very tall**
and holds me up.

But then, just when I'm about to save the day,
another **terrible** thing happens.

Dad tells me not to worry.
"Think about all the **fun** things we've done, Raj!"

I think about our day, and then I remember!
"We were going to take the bus," I say.
"But I have a **better** idea."

"Let's fly home instead!"

"A superhero
duo!"
says Dad.

Finally, we make it home.
"Have you got your keys, Dad?" I say.

Dad looks in his bag. Then he rummages inside.
Then he turns it upside down. I don't see any keys.

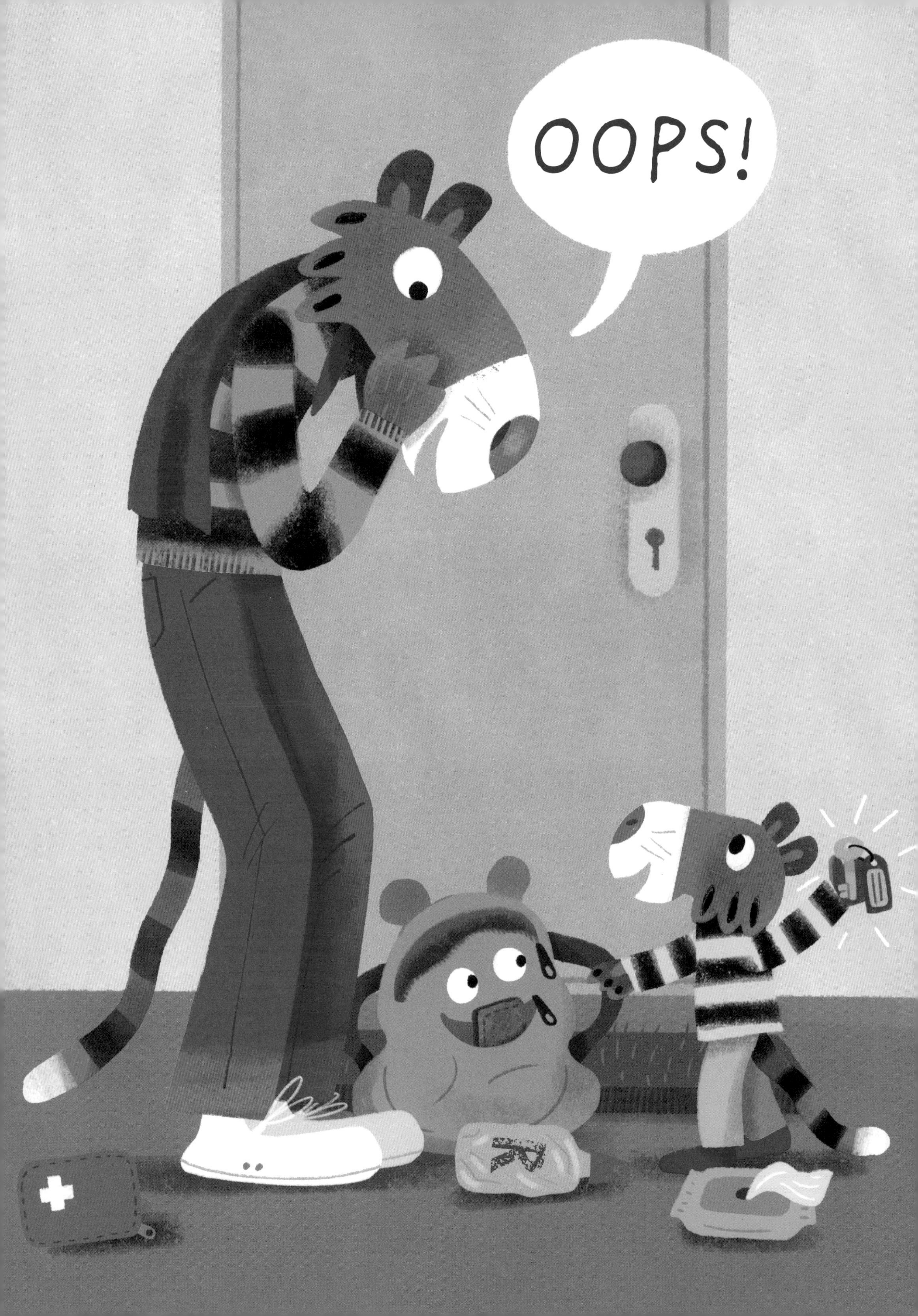
OOPS!

The end !